I0569915

THE WEDDING WISH

By
Ginny Baird

Published by
Winter Wedding Press

Edited by Linda Ingmanson
Cover by Dar Albert

About the Author

From the time that she could talk, romance author Ginny Baird was making up stories, much to the delight—and consternation—of her family and friends. By grade school, she'd turned that inclination into a talent, whereby her teacher allowed her to write and produce plays, rather than write boring book reports. Ginny continued writing throughout college, where she contributed articles to her literary campus weekly, then later pursued a career managing international projects with the US State Department.

Ginny has held an assortment of jobs, including school teacher, freelance fashion model, and greeting card writer, and has published more than ten works of fiction and optioned nine screenplays. She has additionally published short stories, nonfiction and poetry, and admits to being a true romantic at heart.

Ginny is the author of several bestselling romantic comedies, including novellas in her *Holiday Brides Series*. She's a member of Romance Writers of America (RWA), the RWA Published Authors Network (PAN), and Virginia Romance Writers (VRW).

When she's not writing, Ginny enjoys cooking, biking and spending time with her family in Tidewater, Virginia. She loves hearing from her readers and welcomes visitors to her website at http://www.ginnybairdromance.com.

Books by Ginny Baird

Summer Grooms Series
Must-Have Husband
My Lucky Groom
The Wedding Wish

Holiday Brides Series
The Christmas Catch
The Holiday Bride
Mistletoe in Maine
Beach Blanket Santa
The Holiday Brides Collection
(Books 1 - 4)

Other Titles
Real Romance
The Sometime Bride
Santa Fe Fortune
How to Marry a Matador
Real Romance and The Sometime Bride
(Gemini Edition)
Santa Fe Fortune and How to Marry a Matador
(Gemini Edition)

THE WEDDING WISH

TABLE OF CONTENTS

Chapter One

Isabel strolled quickly through central campus, a backpack slung over her shoulder. The backpack bounced as she scurried along, rushing to make her eleven o'clock class. The day was bright and sunny with Frisbee players dotting the green stretch of lawn. Soon spring semester would end, and a lazy summer ambiance would settle in amid the blossoming dogwoods and magnolia trees. She was studying for her Masters in Art so was determined to go straight through her program. Being a year-round student wasn't so bad, and her job in the art library helped her afford it. The grant money didn't hurt either. She'd never really planned to go to school in the same town where her parents lived, but when the financial packages came in, this had been the best offer she'd gotten.

Wham! Isabel felt something slam into her shoulder, and her backpack slid to the ground.

"Oh man! I'm so sorr—"

She looked up into gorgeous brown eyes. He stood about six feet tall, with extra-broad shoulders and honey-blond hair.

His expression lit up. "Isabel? Isabel Miller?"

She paused a moment to study him; then her lips turned up in a grin. It couldn't be, but it was. The one man who'd completely broken her heart. Of course, that had been at age twelve, but still… "Robert?"

His face warmed all over as he held her gaze. "I can't believe it's you."

"Ditto."

He bent quickly to the ground and picked up her backpack, then handed it over. "I totally apologize for running into you. Are you all right?"

"I think so," she said, still dumbstruck. "I mean, yeah. Of course." Robert Reed, after all this time. Since he'd morphed into a man, she was surprised she'd recognized him. Then again, she could never forget those chocolate-colored eyes.

"I hope I didn't leave a bruise."

Oh, he'd left a bruise all right. Way down deep in her heart. But that hadn't really been his fault. "I'm sure I'll live," she said, sliding the backpack onto her shoulder.

"I can't believe you're at Eastern," he said. "Are you a student?"

"Who says you can't go home again?" she asked with a grin. "How about you?"

"I did the same," he told her. "I'm in med school, second year."

She tilted her head to the side, springy curls bouncing. "As I recall, you always had the inclination."

His handsome face colored from the neck up. No doubt, he remembered too. All those late afternoons in the den playing doctor. Mostly what got examined was her mouth—with his tongue. Not that she'd minded. Isabel had actually suggested the game.

Robert stared down into pretty blue eyes, feeling his temperature spike. While he'd believed Isabel to be pretty as a kid, she was one smoking knockout now. Her golden hair still fell in ringlets past her shoulders, but those shoulders now framed an awesomely female body. "Isabel, let me explain…"

She laughed sweetly, the sound recalling a song from long ago. "No explanations needed. Whatever you remember, I had a part in it too."

He fell into her eyes, the sky and trees swirling around him. How could she still do this to him after so much time? "Yes. I mean…" He stammered slightly. "We both did. Want to."

"I sure did," she said, her pretty face aglow.

Robert suddenly remembered his mission. "It's been so great seeing you, but I've got to get somewhere."

Isabel checked the time on her cell. "Me too."

"Where are you headed?"

"To the Art Center. And you?"

His face flamed. "I'm uh…" He glanced quickly around the quad. "Going that way," he said, pointing in the opposite direction. "Say, Isabel," he said before she could turn to go. "Do you think we could meet up later? It would be great to grab a cup of coffee and hear what you've been up to."

Her face brightened in a smile. "Coffee later sounds great."

"Meet me at the Student Center? Three o'clock?"

"Three it is," she said, dashing off.

Isabel took a seat before an easel and pulled a stash of pastel pencils from her backpack.

"You know what I hate about these life drawing classes?" Cindy asked from beside her. "It's the models they get. We're supposed to be talking body form here. Think Michelangelo's David. But all we ever get are these little skinny dudes. Waiflike, if you can even apply that term to guys."

"All bodies are beautiful in their own way." She was glad she'd finally gotten a class with her best friend. This had been the first one all year. During the last session, they'd studied the female figure. Today's focus was the male anatomy. She adjusted her newsprint on the board before her, feeling Cindy grab her arm.

"Hang on," Cindy said under her breath. "I think we've just been blessed."

Isabel slowly raised her eyes to spy the back of their tall, blond model as he slid the robe from his frame. Musculature rippled across his well-toned back and taut derriere. "O. M. G."

"Yeah. Right," Cindy whispered. "I'm almost scared to have him turn around."

As he did, Isabel gasped. When she and Robert had played doctor as kids, they'd teased each other with slight glimpses of each other's bodies, but she'd never seen as much of him as *all that.* Even if she had, it certainly couldn't have competed with the way he looked now. All grown up and gorgeous.

Robert set his robe on a nearby table, then took his place on the stool at the front of the room, bathed in the spotlights' glow. He was...absolutely...perfect. From his head down to his toes then... Oh! All the way back up again—past his buff six-pack and broad, muscled chest and that hot-as-sin sexy face that, in and of itself, could make most women moan. Isabel swallowed hard, not at all sure she could do this.

"What's the matter?" Cindy asked, hastily beginning to sketch. "Why aren't you starting?"

Isabel was grateful she sat at the back of the room and that the glare from the lights was in his eyes. She felt her grip on her pencil slide as her palms went moist.

"I just never thought I'd have this opportunity."

"You and me both," Cindy said, giving Isabel's hand holding the pencil a nudge. "And neither of us is going to waste it."

"No," Isabel said, striving to remain professional. "I wouldn't dream of it."

Robert sat as still as possible, trying to distract himself from the fact that he was sitting naked before a crowded room. If he hadn't made that deal with his buddy Alan, he'd never be here. As it was, he was stuck upholding his end of the bargain. When he'd been suddenly called out of town to New York, he'd needed someone to pick up his shift at the lab quickly. The sole volunteer in sight had been Alan—although Alan's offer of help had come with a price. He had a freelance job he needed Robert's help with later. Robert had easily agreed, thinking maybe Alan did part-time landscaping or something. He had no clue he'd wind up here, like Adam in need of a fig leaf.

Robert's only sense of relief lay in believing nobody in the class knew him. He'd just caught a glimpse of their faces as he'd entered the studio, and, gratefully, none had looked familiar. Now all he had to do was stay put for the next ninety minutes, ignoring the fact that his...uh...personal attributes were on open display. The fact was, there was nothing personal about this. This was a centuries' old practice concerning the rendering of art and creative portrayals of the human body. That it was his body in particular didn't matter one iota to any of the artists in the room. And Robert knew he'd do well to remember that.

Robert approached the Student Center, spying a beautiful blonde seated in a booth beside the plate-glass window. A backpack was parked beside her on the bench as she busily tapped at the laptop positioned before her on the table. She worked with fierce concentration, oblivious to the swirl of commotion around her. The Student Center was always a busy place, with people bustling in and out, chatting loudly and carrying coffee. The young woman was wholesome-looking yet refined. There was something so familiar about the curve of her cheek... Robert reached for the door, and she turned toward him and smiled. His heart leapt in his chest. *Isabel*. She was even prettier than he'd recalled her being on the lawn. And his memory should still be sharp. That was only four hours ago.

Blue eyes met his and twinkled. "I was beginning to think you'd stood me up," she said in a soft Southern twang that made the back of his neck flash hot. Isabel and her family had moved here from Atlanta when she was just ten. She'd never fully lost the accent. Even as a kid, Robert had found the sweet cadence of her words intoxicating. He took a seat across from her in the booth, noting he still wasn't immune to her charms. "I'm a man of my word," he assured her, settling his own backpack in place. "I hope you haven't been waiting long?"

"Just a few minutes. But that's okay. Been checking my new class schedule."

"For the fall?"

"Summer session, actually."

"No kidding? I'll be here too."

Their eyes locked for a heated moment.

Even though it was so long ago, the memory of their first kiss seemed like yesterday. Robert bringing his ineffectual mouth to hers. Of all things, wearing braces! He'd been so inept, she'd nearly bitten his tongue. Not that he'd blamed her entirely. Even then, he knew he'd probably deserved it, as awkward in his approach as he was.

"It's a little warm out for coffee," she said. "I think I'll grab a soda. Can I get one for you?"

"Uh, yeah. I mean, no." He felt his temperature spike again and wondered if there was something wrong with the AC in here. Robert shifted on the bench, extracting his wallet. "I'll get both of ours. My treat."

She reached in her backpack and handed him her perma-refill tumbler. "I've got the enviro-friendly cup. Hope you don't mind."

"Very ecological of you," he said, taking it from her.

He quickly cleared his throat, thinking he must look like an idiot. Flustered by some ridiculous reverie more than a decade old. "I've got to tell you, Isabel, you look terrific. How long has it been?"

"Oh gosh, has to have been at least…sixteen years!" She studied him a moment, then delicately arched an eyebrow. "And I mean it quite sincerely when I say you look fantastic too. Totally…buff."

"How was your class?" he asked, hearing his voice grow froggy.

She pinned him in place with pretty blue eyes. "Revealing. And yours?"

He stood so quickly, his knees knocked the table. "Uh, no, I wasn't in class," he said, starting to walk away.

"Really?"

He nearly stumbled over his own feet walking backward. "Let's just say I had a debt to repay." If Isabel hadn't been in that studio, why was she eyeing him so suspiciously? Like she could see right through him, or at the very least clear down to his skin.

"Are you okay?" she asked as he nearly collided with another student.

He shot her a tight smile. "Fine. Just fine. Diet drink should help."

Isabel watched him walk away, thinking a man with his physique didn't need to worry about *diet anything*. And she should know. She'd just studied him in incredible detail. He headed for the drink dispenser, glancing over his shoulder with a tense smile. Why was he on edge all of a sudden? He'd seemed just fine when they'd run into each other outdoors. Could it be he'd seen her sitting in the art studio? Practically drooling in the far recesses of the class? Isabel noted Robert had jammed her cup below the ice dispenser, but his eyes were still glued on hers. She watched wide-eyed as ice spewed forth and began to tumble over the rim of the cup.

Robert stared down in horror at the cascading display. He yanked on the cup, but it wouldn't budge, wedged somehow between the back of the machine and the lip of the dispenser. Something inside the ice machine started churning loudly as ice began to *spit...spit...spit...*past the jammed tumbler and onto the floor. Robert grabbed the cup with both hands and yanked hard, his face crimson from the neck up. Isabel glanced around the room and raced to his rescue, wrapping her hands around his on the icy cup. "I can't move it," he grated between clenched teeth as the machine whirred louder, burying his loafers in cascading ice.

"I'll help!" she called above the commotion as others in the Student Center gathered to stare. She tightened her fingers around his, leaning back to give herself leverage. "On go!"

"Go?"

"Ready… Set…"

"Gotcha!

"Go!"

They pulled hard together, and the cup jerked free. Isabel fell back on her bottom as Robert slid to his knees beside her, and an icy avalanche ensued, pinging them both with constant fury. Robert grabbed a cafeteria tray from a nearby shelf, shielding them both from the onslaught. As he reached a hand toward Isabel to help her stand, a hefty woman pushed past them. "Excuse me!" The university worker in a hairnet with big, burly arms strode straight to the machine and hit the ice dispenser button—hard. The machine whined to a halt, and the ice assault stopped, finishing with three little spews of cubes near the end.

"Are you okay?" Robert turned his eyes on Isabel as she stood on shaky knees, the ground beneath them crunching. She couldn't help but see the absurdity of the moment, nor its irony either.

"I was just thinking." She gave a wry twist to her lips and surveyed him soundly. "Now that we've broken the ice between us, maybe we should have dinner?"

He laughed lightly, his face awash with relief as he dabbed his damp clothing with napkins. He handed a stack to her, and she did the same. "Dinner sounds great. What did you have in mind?"

"I was thinking of taking you home to see my parents," she said, knowing as she did the idea seemed right. They'd invited her over this evening anyway. Naturally, they'd be happy to see an old family friend.

"Are you sure? It's kind of late notice."

"Don't be silly," she said, swatting his shoulder with the side of her cup. "My folks will welcome you with open arms."

Chapter Two

Kip pulled back the door with a broad grin beneath his bushy moustache. "Baby," he said in his deep Southern drawl. "Welcome home!"

He paused momentarily, narrowing his gaze at Robert. "You, on the other hand," he said with a dismissive look, "can stay outside. Or go home altogether. Whatever it is you're peddling, we don't want any." He began to press his hand toward Robert's chest, but Isabel pushed it away.

"Daddy! I'm surprised at you. This is Robert. Robert Reed. Don't you remember?"

Kip took a step forward and assessed Robert with an appraising frown. "Robert? Little Robert? *Nooo.*"

Trudy brushed past him, squealing with glee. "Well, look what the cat dragged in! Robert Reed, of all people!" Her blonde bob bounced as she wrapped him in a tight hug, then pulled back with an appreciative smile. "And all grown up too." She nudged her husband with her elbow. "Just look at him, Kip. It's almost hard to believe he's the same boy."

"Hmm, yes. Hard to believe at that." As far as Kip recalled, Robert had been buck-toothed and scrawny. And—this part hadn't slipped his mind—forever angling to get his hands on Isabel. He'd developed the sneaking suspicion that little Isabel was becoming interested in Robert too. He'd come home from work early one afternoon and had discovered them playing some sort of parlor game that involved both of them lying down on the sofa. When Robert's dad had been transferred to another position up north, Kip had been more than relieved. He'd been ecstatic. A preteen girl was hard enough to handle without a boy with raging hormones living next door. And Kip knew a thing or two about hormones. He'd been a young man once himself.

Robert nodded politely at them both. "Mr. and Mrs. Miller, it's really great to see you." He extended his hand toward Kip, but Kip just stared at it like it was some frightening harbinger from his past. *What on earth is the boy doing here? After all this time? And how come my dear daughter looks like she's already got stars in her eyes? Didn't she just break up with a boyfriend? Okay. So maybe that was two or three years ago... But still, a woman's tender heart needs time to heal.*

"Kip..." Trudy urged in a sing-songy voice, her grin tight across those pearly whites.

"Oh, right." He shook Robert's hand. Extra firmly, to remind him Kip was the man in charge. If Robert was up to no good at thirteen, who knew what kind of trouble he could brew as an adult man?

"Where are our manners?" Trudy said brightly. "Robert, Isabel, please come inside." Then, to Kip's horror, she turned to Robert and said she hoped he'd join them for dinner. While women prided themselves on intuition, Kip's manly instincts had never failed him. They'd gotten him by in business and had helped him become one of the area's most lucrative contractors. It helped that he'd developed a keen sense about who to trust and who not to. Robert Reed had always been on Kip's *not to* list. And until Robert did something stellar to change his mind, Kip was standing by his first impression.

Trudy excused herself to go check something in the kitchen as Kip settled his gaze on Robert's. "Can I fix you something to drink?" he asked in a perfunctory tone that said he'd have preferred it better if Robert hadn't stayed at all.

Isabel grinned sweetly at her dad, oblivious to the whole thing. "I'll have some wine, thanks. White, if you have it."

Robert had chalked up his memories of Mr. Miller as a big, old grizzly bear to youthful imagination. Now he wondered if that recollection wasn't squarely on target.

"I'll have what she's having," he told Mr. Miller, in an effort to be conciliatory. Robert didn't want any trouble here. But he did want to spend time with Isabel. And if that meant also spending time with her family... Well then, Robert would just have to man up and do it. Mrs. Miller was pleasant enough to deal with anyway. Robert was certain all of Isabel's good qualities must have been inherited from her.

The older man huffed and strode away, hands jammed in his pockets.

Once he was out of earshot, Robert turned toward Isabel with a grimace. "I'm not so sure my coming here was a good idea."

"Why on earth not?"

"I don't think your dad is so happy to see me."

"Oh, come on! He's just a big, old teddy bear!"

"Grizzly's more like it."

"Okay," she said in a whisper. "I'll admit he sometimes comes off a little gruff. But his bark is worse than his bite."

Robert pursed his lips and said nothing.

"Just give him some time to get to know you again."

"That's what I mean. He never liked me in the first place!"

"Who told you that?"

"You did."

She covered her mouth with a giggle. "I did, didn't I? Well, that wasn't very nice. I probably shouldn't have. And whether or not that was true... That was all those years ago. You're a grown man now. I'm sure my dad sees you differently."

Robert swallowed hard, hoping that was so. It felt so great seeing Isabel again and being in her company. After they'd made an icy mess of the Student Center—and had helped to clean it up again—they'd sat, laughing and talking over old times for hours. In some ways, it had been like stepping right back in time to a faraway place that was nearly forgotten yet familiar. Isabel was lighthearted and fun to talk to, and, not so incidentally, extremely easy on the eyes. If she hadn't had this previous engagement with her folks, he would have asked her out himself. That would have been nice too, to be able to continue their earlier conversation—alone.

"Darling," Kip said, reappearing and handing his daughter a glass before offering another to Robert. "I hope you like Chardonnay. It's one of the local varieties, one of our best."

Robert took an appreciative sip and nodded in approval. "It's perfect, thanks."

Trudy emerged from the kitchen with a sunny smile. "You're in luck, Robert. The new dishes I'm trying are plenty enough for four." She gave a little swivel to her hips beneath her prim A-line skirt and matching blouse and summer sweater. "Cooking *Caribe,* anyone?"

As Robert and Isabel trailed her parents into the dining room, Isabel warned Robert. "Prepare yourself," she said under her breath. "Trudy's on a new cuisine-from-around-the-world kick. Last time, it was fried goat's head."

"I'm sure I can handle it," Robert said with a chuckle.

Isabel shot him a quizzical look.

"I'm in med school, remember?" he returned in low tones. "Nothing I could see would shock me."

Thirty minutes later, Trudy held the brimming platter in his direction. "More *plátanos,* Robert?"

He stared down at the enormous glazed bananas, that—for the life of him—looked like caramelized parts of the male anatomy. "Um, no... Thanks. They're delicious, though."

Isabel shot Robert a coquettish smile. "I'll take some more," she said, reaching for the platter. "I don't think I could get enough."

Kip leaned forward and took the platter from Trudy, setting it on the table beside him. "Perhaps you've already had enough."

"But I love these! Don't you, Mom?"

Trudy sliced into hers with gusto, and Robert winced. "They're to die for."

Kip took the napkin from his lap and splayed it open, covering the offending bananas.

Trudy cocked her chin at him from the other end of the table.

"So, tell me," Kip said, addressing Robert. "How is it you ran into Isabel again?"

"We bumped into each other on campus today," Robert said, preparing to take another bite of pork *piñon*.

"Yes," Isabel quipped. "Didn't I tell you? He has the most liberating job at the Art Center."

Trudy's brow rose with interest. "Liberating, how?"

Robert's fork fell to his plate with a *clank*.

"Is that where you saw each other?" Kip asked, perplexed. He turned to Robert. "But I thought you were in medical school?"

"I...am," Robert stammered, suddenly overheated.

Isabel gave him an impish look. "In some ways, it was like no time had gone by..." she mused. "In others, it was like seeing him for the very first time."

Kip peered under the napkin at the plantains, then narrowed his gaze at his daughter.

Isabel widened her eyes at Robert and sat up straighter as if to contain herself from bursting out laughing. Robert could tell she was having fun with this, razzing him in front of her folks like she used to do as a kid.

"What is it you do at the Art Center, Robert?" Trudy asked.

"I'm afraid that's all a big misunderstanding," he said, avoiding Isabel's gaze. "Actually, I work at the lab."

"I see," Trudy said, obviously confused.

Kip made an effort to redirect the conversation. "How's your family?"

"My parents are fine, sir. Thanks for asking."

"And your sister, Teresa?"

"Working in New York in publishing."

"How nice."

"Yes, my folks are very proud of her. We all are."

"Is she married?" Trudy queried politely.

Robert nodded. "To her high school sweetheart."

"That's sweet," Trudy said. "Was it an old love rekindled, or have they been together the whole time?"

Robert's eyes fell on Isabel, who watched him intently.

"They've been together ever since the tenth grade."

"You see, Kip. Things like that *can* last." Then, by way of explanation, she said to Robert, "My husband's always saying they can't. That people who fall in love young don't stay together."

"Just look at Romeo and Juliet," Kip said. "You can't say that didn't spell disaster."

"That was a play, Daddy," Isabel said.

"Ah! But fiction mimics life. Isn't that what you always say, dear?" he asked Trudy.

Her mouth fell open. "That's not what I meant, and you know it."

"Don't mind him," Isabel said to Robert, regarding her father. "Daddy doesn't have a romantic bone in his body."

"That's patently untrue," Kip protested. "Just ask your mother what I got her for our last anniversary. Go on, ask."

Trudy sighed. "Very lovely season tickets… To the Chargers basketball games."

"I rest my case," Kip said proudly. "Can't get any more romantic than that!"

Trudy shook her head at her husband, but Robert could tell it was in fondness. Despite his foibles, Mrs. Miller still apparently adored her husband. "Do Teresa and her husband have children?" she asked.

"They've got two now, with one on the way."

"And you?" Kip prodded. "You're a few years older, but never...?"

"Dad," Isabel admonished, "that's really none of our business."

"Why not?

"Because, it's... You know." She shrugged. "Personal."

"Well, I don't know what's so personal about it. An old friend of the family shows up here. I want to know about his life. There's no reason he wouldn't tell me." He gave Robert a pointed stare. "Unless he's got something to hide. *Ouch!*" He reached down under the table to rub his shin, the one that Trudy had apparently just kicked.

"Let me get some of these plates out of the way," Trudy said, standing. She glanced around at their faces. "Then I can serve coffee, if you'd like."

"Sit back down, Trudy," Kip commanded. "We're not finished yet."

"I think Mom's right," Isabel began.

Robert slowly raised a hand, then met all of their eyes. "It's okay. I don't mind talking about it." He paused, then spoke to Kip. "The truth is, sir, there was somebody. Somebody special, but as things sometimes happen, they didn't work out. Perhaps, as you say, we started too young."

"I'm sorry," Isabel murmured apologetically from across the table. "Daddy, you really shouldn't have."

Trudy shook her head sympathetically. "Isabel knows just what that's like. She and her boyfriend broke up too."

"*Mo-om.* That was four years ago."

Robert studied her a beat. "I'm sorry for you too."

"Seriously," she said, flustered, "I'm over it."

"He was a very nice boy too," Trudy went on.

"Nope." Kip shook his head. "Couldn't trust him. You know how he did that shifty thing with his eyes?"

"Daddy!" Isabel said. "He wore contacts."

"That was a handy excuse."

"The truth is," Trudy said, "he did turn out to be a bad apple."

Isabel's expression grew long. "He cheated on me."

Silence settled over the table as Robert held Isabel's gaze. If there was one thing Robert knew for sure, it was that, if he had someone like Isabel, he'd never look at another woman. "Then he must have been a fool."

"He certainly was." Kip stood beside his wife. "Here, let me help with those dishes. That is," he said, turning toward the others, "if everybody's done?"

"I'm done," Isabel said softly.

"Me too," Robert said, still lost in her gaze. But in an odd sort of way, he felt like things between them were just beginning.

A short time later, Robert and Isabel stood on the stoop outside her apartment building, saying good night.

"I had a really good time at dinner," he told her. "Thanks for including me."

"You stood up to my Dad's grilling pretty well. Thanks for indulging him and being so polite."

"I understand he cares about you."

"Yeah."

"I know what that's like."

Isabel stared up into gorgeous brown eyes, remembering what it was like caring for Robert. As a kid, she'd more than cared for him. She'd had a raging crush. And, by the way her pulsed raced each time he looked in her eyes, she wasn't sure she was over it.

"Isabel," he said, as moonlight hovered up above and a light breeze blew. "Do you think we could...? What I mean is, would you like to do this again? Dinner sometime? Just the two of us?"

She felt her cheeks warm. "Just the two of us sounds fine."

"It will probably be less eventful that way."

"Maybe," she said with a saucy lilt to her voice. "Then again, it could get tricky."

"Tricky?" He grinned, and her heart went all aflutter.

"Who knows what could happen with the two of us left alone?"

"We used to get into quite a bit of trouble," he agreed, stepping closer. Memories tugged her back over the years and into his arms. They were lanky then, but muscled now. Toned enough to pull her close, pressing his all-grown-up body to hers. If only he would hold her, she would let him. Just to relive that old feeling once again. "And something tells me your dad hasn't forgotten."

"Maybe he sees you differently now."

"What do you see?" he asked, looking down at her.

"I like what I see." Her eyes lingered on his. "And I've seen quite a lot."

When he spoke, his voice was raspy. "Oh man, I can't believe you were in that studio. I'm sorry you had to see that."

"You don't have to apologize to me," she said softly. "The human body's very beautiful in all its dimensions." Robert's in particular, though she wasn't prepared to say so.

"It wasn't what you think."

"I don't care."

"You didn't mind it? Seeing me that way?"

"Robert. I'm an artist, a professional. One body is the same as the next," she lied.

"Hmm. I'm not sure if I could say the same, were you the patient and me the doctor."

"I believe we've been there and done that."

"Yeah," he said with a wistful look. "I would have done it more, but your dad always walked in on us."

"Robert!" she said with a laugh. "That's probably why he didn't like you."

"It's most certainly why he didn't like me. I'd likely have reacted the same about my own daughter."

"Something tells me you'll be a little more laid back about parenting."

"Might somewhat depend."

"On what?"

"Whether I have boys or girls."

"Go on!" She shot him a smile, enjoying their banter. How she wished it could continue and that this evening wouldn't have to end.

"Isabel?"

"Huh?"

"Would you mind if showed you something?"

"Aren't we a little old for that?" she teased.

"We're not too old for this." He reached forward and lightly thumbed her nose, the way he used to do when they were kids, and her heart hammered harder. "Spend a few more minutes with me, Isabel. There's something I'd really like you to see."

Robert had been having so much fun with Isabel, he hadn't been ready for their time together to end. Seeing her again was like stepping into a time warp, where a crazy jumble of emotions came tumbling back. He knew they'd just been kids, but a guy didn't easily forget his first love—even if he loved her at age thirteen. Robert had been one year older and a year ahead in school. It had made him feel important at the time, like he was older and wiser. Although in truth, Isabel often had the upper hand. She was quick on the uptake and enjoyed catching him off guard with a fast turn of phrase or daring challenge. Like the time she dared him to share a piece of gum by passing it back and forth between them using only their tongues.

"We're going back?" she asked in surprise. They'd just cleared the entrance to her parents' neighborhood, which was situated high on a hill above the city.

"In a way," he said with a mysterious smile. "But probably not to where you think."

A few minutes later, Robert turned up a steep gravel road, then pulled off to the side.

"You're taking me parking?" she asked. Though in truth she didn't look opposed.

He shot her a sly wink before exiting the car. "You're so suspicious." Robert opened her door, extending his hand. "Come on."

She scrutinized his face for a moment before accepting. "Where exactly are you taking me?"

"Someplace special," he assured her. "So special, in fact, I've never shown it to anybody else."

Robert held on to her hand and led her up a high path that wound its way past laurels and big briar bushes. "Watch your step," he cautioned. "It's rocky."

Her sneaker slipped sideways, and she stumbled. He spun quickly to catch her, holding her in his arms. "It's okay. I've got you."

She looked up at him, and it was all he could do to resist bringing his mouth to hers. "Thank you."

"For what?"

"For this. For whatever it is you're doing. I have no clue where we're going, but this is fun. I feel like I'm just a kid who's snuck out of her room."

"Oh yeah? Well, I'm about to show you where I went when I snuck out of mine."

Before Isabel knew it, Robert had led her through the shadows and up upon a flat-topped rock overlooking the city. An array of lights twinkled below as warm summer breezes blew. Isabel caught her breath at the sight. "It's beautiful."

"Yeah." Robert drew his arm around her and held her close. "I used to spend a lot of time up here as a kid. Thinking."

"Oh? What did you think about?" She turned toward him.

"You, mostly."

"Me?"

"All right, maybe I didn't have the guts to tell you then, but I'm man enough to own it now…" His eyes twinkled in the faint glow of lights from the distant city. "I had the most unbearable crush on this pretty, blonde-haired girl."

Isabel felt her face warm. "That's funny," she said, looking up at him. "The feeling was mutual."

"Yeah?"

"Yeah." She turned toward the view, avoiding his gaze. "I cried for weeks after you left. Did you know that? Weeks and weeks. Really. I think you were the first man to totally break my heart."

He reached up and gently stroked her cheek. "If it had been up to me, I never would have gone."

"I know," she said quietly.

They both stood staring at the view as warm summer winds rippled around them.

"You want to stay for a while?" he asked. "Just sit here with me?"

"I'd like that."

And so they stayed, and they talked. And then they talked some more over old times and all the fun they used to have until they finally ran out of words, and the sun broke over the horizon.

Chapter Three

Isabel smiled brightly as they exited the movie theater. "I just love a good romantic comedy, don't you?" She looked so pretty tonight in worn blue jeans and a light blue top that complemented her eyes. Robert didn't think he'd ever been out with anyone better looking or nicer to be with. Being in Isabel's company just felt right.

"I like 'em if you do," Robert told her.

She nudged him lightly as they strolled down the sidewalk amid the clutter of shops and outdoor cafés. "What's that supposed to mean?"

"That means I'm remembering our deal."

"That we watch an action film next?"

"Exactly."

"You drive a hard bargain, mister." There was a happy lilt to her voice, like she was enjoying herself. Robert was having a great time too. How he wished there could be more between them and that all those loose ends from his past were neatly tied up.

"Want to grab some pizza?" he queried.

"Only if I get to order extra pepperoni."

"Anything your heart desires."

Her eyes sparkled in the soft glow from the streetlights. "You should watch what you're offering."

"What do you mean?"

"I might just ask for anchovies too."

Robert wasn't much for anchovies, but he didn't care. He'd eat anything at all that Isabel wanted. Hell, he'd even watch another chick flick too. Anything to be around her.

"That'll be fine," he said without skipping a beat. "Just as long as we get to wash them down with beer."

"Why, Robert," she said, flirting. "Are you aiming to get me drunk and take advantage of me?"

Get her drunk? Never. Take advantage? Boy, I'd like to. Or at the very least, I'd like to let her take advantage of me. Robert sighed inwardly, wishing life weren't so messy and that everything was as light and breezy as being with Isabel made it seem. But he had stuff to deal with. Serious stuff. And, goodness knew, he was working on it. "You keep flirting with me that way," he told her, "you're going to get yourself into a lot of trouble someday."

She gasped in shock, but Robert could tell she was pretending. "That would be a shame," she said with a giggle. "A terrible, horrible shame."

He studied her a moment. "Yeah. Wouldn't it, though?"

But to Isabel's disappointment, he didn't kiss her later that night. Even despite the fact that they'd shared a whole pitcher of beer. She didn't understand what precisely was going on between them. All she knew was that it felt good. She liked being around Robert, and they always had a super time. She simply wasn't sure why he hadn't taken things to the next level. She'd considered making a bold move herself, but then had thought better of it. Maybe the timing wasn't good, if he wasn't ready. What was the point in rushing things when everything was going so well with the slow build that they had going on? Pizza and a movie had only been their second date anyway. If things kept going the way they had been, she'd find herself in Robert's arms before she knew it. Then the scrumptious doctor-to-be would have to look out. He'd be the one undergoing the thorough examination. Isabel blushed at the billion dirty thoughts racing through her mind as Robert told her good night.

"I had a lot of fun," he said.

"Yeah," she agreed. "Tonight was great."

"Can we do it again?"

"Any time. Just text me."

He hesitated a moment, but then stepped back.

"I think I'll call."

"Why's that?"

A slow grin spread across his face. "I like the sound of your voice."

Trudy turned toward Kip and set her hands on her hips. She stood in the kitchen, where she'd been shelving cookbooks in alphabetical order, sorted by geographical region. Kip sat at the table, hiding behind his newspaper, but he spied her watching him over the top of it just the same.

"I don't know what you have against Robert," she said, growing agitated. "He's a nice young man now, and Isabel seems to have taken an interest in him."

Kip grunted and thumbed through the sports section. "Her interest in Robert's not new. Neither is his in her."

"Oh, come now, Kip. You can't tell me you haven't gotten over that sofa thing."

Kip stared at his wife. "He was practically on top of her!"

"So? They were experimenting."

"You're not helping, Trudy."

"Honey, they were just kids."

"Yes. And maybe Robert's family moving away was a blessing. There was always something about that boy. Something not quite right."

"You're just being an overprotective father."

"That's not true."

She cocked her chin and got that little pout to her mouth that said she thought it was. "All I'm saying is that your daughter's twenty-eight now. Old enough to make up her own mind."

"I still didn't like the way he said it."

"Said *what*?"

"That thing about his past relationship."

"You were being intrusive."

"No. I was being inquisitive. There's a difference."

"What's the difference?"

"Inquisitive only becomes intrusive when the other party's got something to hide."

"Kip! For heaven's sake."

"Fine, fine." He rattled his paper in front of him. "Isabel's a big girl like you say. Just don't expect me to pick up the pieces…"

Trudy strode over and snatched away his paper.

His mouth hung open. "Just what are you doing?"

"Taking away your shield so I can bop you over the head with it."

With that, she rolled up the paper and popped him on his crown.

"Ouch!"

"Grow up, Kip," she said, handing him back his paper. "And think up something better to do than obsess about your only daughter."

"Only child," he corrected as she walked away.

Trudy waved one hand in the air and strode out the door, leaving Kip alone with his thoughts, and—*oh no, not that*—a totally torn sports section.

Isabel lowered her menu in front of her after having perused the delicious selections. She and Robert were out on yet another date. They'd seen each other every Saturday for the past several weeks and lots of weekdays in between. Most nights, they both were studying, and on Fridays, Robert worked late at the lab. "Everything looks so good," she told him. "I'm having trouble making up my mind."

"I'll probably have the porter house steak," he told her. "With an order of jalapeño fries on the side." That sounded great, and Isabel was tempted, but there was also a lovely sounding salmon.

"I'm thinking of the fish."

"Then why not go for it? If you want to do surf and turf, we can share."

The solution sounded perfect, but before she could say so, Robert's cell rang.

"I'm sorry, Isabel," he said, checking the number. "I'd better take this."

She used the opportunity to excuse herself to the rest room. She needed to avail herself of the facilities and wanted to check her makeup besides. She'd taken care to look good, and Robert seemed to appreciate her. But it was odd that he'd still not tried to make a move. He'd certainly been much more forward as a kid. Then again, she probably had been too. Now it seemed they were being adults about it. Taking their time to get to know one another, although Isabel couldn't help but feel their getting-to-know-each-other period was well past done. They'd been on at least half a dozen nighttime dates, and Robert always insisted on paying. And yet, each time he'd driven her home, he'd played the perfect gentleman. Isabel worried over why he was keeping his distance. Could it be he was so caught up in school, he wasn't prepared to become intimately involved? Or maybe it was her, and he didn't feel romantically inclined. Perhaps he merely thought of them as good friends, with a fond past as childhood sweethearts? The only other explanation was that he was seeing someone else, but that certainly seemed impossible. Robert appeared to have very limited time, and what free time he had he seemed to want to spend with her. Besides, he'd pretty clearly indicated to her dad there *was no one else.* At least that there hadn't been for quite some time.

Isabel entered the rest room to find two young women chatting busily while applying lipstick before the mirror. "That's what I'm telling you," the first one said to the other, clearly upset. "When a guy's got something to hide, he always says that."

"That's not true," the other protested. "He could have meant anything by it."

"*You too?*" the first one said with emphasis. "I don't think so, girlfriend. He was talking to another woman. He just didn't want you to know it."

"So maybe it was his mother?"

The second girl firmly shook her head. "And he wasn't talking about the rock band either." She capped her lipstick and tucked it back in her purse, fluffing her hair. "Trust me on this. Whoever it was on the other end of that line, she's your very worst nightmare."

"And why's that?" her friend asked defensively.

"Because *she's* already got her hooks in your man."

Both girls suddenly wheeled on Isabel, noticing she'd been eavesdropping.

"Uh," she began uncertainly, "are you two in line?"

"No, uh-huh," they said, scooting out of her way. They huddled together in a whisper while walking toward the door, but Isabel overheard them anyway.

"Did you see how she was listening to us?" the second one said.

"Yeah," the first girl agreed. "I'll bet she's got the same problem."

Isabel returned to the table, feeling disconcerted. She didn't know why some random conversation in the ladies' room had bothered her, but it had. As she drew near the table, Robert was finishing his call. He spied her approaching, then quickly wrapped it up. "Yeah," he said into the mouthpiece with a hasty glance in Isabel's direction. "You too."

He hit End Call, and Isabel's heart rose in her throat. "Everything all right?" she asked, taking her seat as casually as possible.

"Just fine." He fixed his eyes on his menu, but his face seemed to take on a slightly deeper hue. "You wanted the fish, you said?"

A waiter in a bow tie surfaced to take their orders. After checking with Isabel and receiving her consent, Robert also asked for a few more glasses of wine. Why did he look uneasy? As if she'd caught him doing something he shouldn't have.

"Who was that on the phone?" Isabel asked as the maître d' arrived to pour their merlot.

"Just somebody from New York," he said with a distant air. "Say, Isabel. Do you think that tomorrow we could—?"

"Somebody who?" she asked, stopping him.

"Really doesn't matter," he said flatly. "It was business."

But Isabel couldn't imagine what sort of business might take place on a weekend and at this hour. "I see," she said, hearing the hurt tinge her voice.

Robert stretched his hand across the table and held hers. "I don't want you to worry," he said, meeting her gaze. "Worry about anything."

But the fact that he said it only troubled her all the more. "I'm not sure I know what you're saying."

"Just that things have a way of working out. When they're meant to." He lightly squeezed her hand, but she withdrew it.

"A light tomato bisque to start?" the server said, setting their soups in front of them.

"Yes, thanks," Robert rejoined, avoiding Isabel's gaze.

Isabel knew then that whatever was going on, Robert wasn't about to let her in on it. She didn't know why and she didn't know what. But he was hiding something from her, all right. Something gnawed at her, saying her dad had been correct in his assessment yet again. She had the same niggling sensation now that she'd had with her last boyfriend, the one who'd run around on her. After him, she hadn't become involved with anyone on more than just a casual basis. It had hurt too much being lied to and misused that way. She'd thought it would take a lifetime to get over it. But when she'd seen Robert again, everything had changed. Her heart had finally begun to open up and let somebody in. And now that somebody was about to sock her in the gut.

Fire welled in her throat as she tried to push her doubts away, but they fought…and kicked…and clambered their way back up to the surface, making her head spin with all the nauseating possibilities. Isabel willed her eyes not to water, but they did anyhow.

"If you'll excuse me a minute," she said, pushing back in her chair and stepping away. And then she hightailed it into the bathroom, where she yanked out a wad of paper towels and bawled into them like a baby.

Chapter Four

Cindy took a bite of her pastrami on rye and chewed thoughtfully. "Well, I guess there are two ways to look at it," she finally said. "Either he's hiding something from you, or he's not."

They sat in The College Deli, a local establishment not too far from the central campus grounds. "Of course he's hiding something," Isabel answered. "It's just like my dad said." She picked at her salad, then set it aside, suddenly not hungry. "*That Robert Reed can't be trusted,*" she said, echoing her dad's deep baritone.

"You know what I think?" Cindy said, dabbing her mouth with a napkin. "I think you're getting yourself all worked up over something that may not even be. Why not just ask him?"

"I did ask him. That's what I'm trying to tell you. He was evasive at best."

"So, maybe it really was about business."

"What business would that be? Robert's in medical school, not employed by some Fortune 500 company."

Cindy met her eyes. "I guess I kind of see your point. But what would he have to hide?"

"Another woman?"

Cindy paused a beat to consider this. "Well, what's he been like with you?"

"What do you mean?"

"You know *exactly* what I mean." Her lips turned up in a naughty grin. "Is the Statue of David as raging-hot up close and personal as it was under that spotlight?"

Isabel shrugged sadly. "I wouldn't know."

"What?" Cindy reached out and touched her elbow. "You can't mean—"

"Not even a good-night kiss."

"Wow."

"Yeah, totally. Right? What's up with that?" Isabel self-consciously twisted a lock of hair around her index finger. "Do you think it's me?"

Cindy choked on her sweet tea. "Are you kidding me? You listen up, girlfriend. You present quite a package. And I'm not just talking the body. I mean the mind, and the great sense of humor, and the way you can make almost anybody feel at ease. It's definitely not you."

Isabel appreciated that her friend was being so kind, but if it *wasn't* her, then what was it? Only one explanation remained. Okay, maybe two.

Cindy widened her eyes. "He's not...? I mean, could it be he's simply not into women?"

Isabel sighed. "I don't get that vibe from him at all. In fact, the vibe I get is that he *is* into me. Only he never wants to act on it."

"Hmm."

"Yeah. It's strange."

"Well, this can't go on forever," Cindy told her. "You know how relationships are. They either move forward, or they blow apart."

"Unless he thinks of us as just friends."

"You just said you didn't get that vibe."

"No."

"Maybe there *is* someone else."

"Yeah."

"I think you should come right out and ask him."

Isabel felt a twisting inside her telling her that if she did, she might not like the answer. The more time she spent with Robert, the more she realized she liked him. *Liked* maybe even wasn't the right word. Robert was smart, generous and fun to be around, and, goodness knew, unbearably handsome. The hard fact was Isabel was becoming desperately attracted—and way too attached to the idea of forming an involvement with him for more than just the short term.

When she'd been a young girl, spending her life with Robert was all she could dream of. Someday they'd no longer be kids. They'd be grown-ups, with real jobs and big plans. Plans that concerned them settling down and building a family together. Each time her mom had dragged her to another neighborhood wedding, little Isabel had come home with a piece of wedding cake to tuck under her pillow. Superstition said that the man you dreamed of was the man you would marry. But Isabel only ever dreamed of one boy. She'd forgotten all about those dreams and early feelings until she'd started getting to know Robert again. And now that those old emotions had returned, they'd arrived in full force. Isabel could no more stop her heart from falling for Robert than she could halt a runaway train. "But what...?" Her lips trembled. She pressed them together to steady them. "What if he says that there is? That there is someone else?"

Cindy laid a hand on her arm to comfort her. "Then, it's better to know now. Don't you think?"

Isabel met her best friend's eyes, knowing Cindy was right. "It really stinks being a grown-up sometimes."

"I know it does," Cindy said, leaning forward. "But at least we can be grown-ups together." Her face was etched with sympathy. "And if he gives you bad news, I don't want you to think your world has ended. Because, let's face it, Isabel, you're a great girl. Plus, you've got your whole life ahead of you… A career. A future. And someday, yes, someday, you're going to find a way to share it with the perfect guy."

Isabel felt like she'd already found the perfect guy. Perfect for her in so many ways. The only question was, did Robert feel the same way about her?

Early the following Sunday morning, Isabel found herself at the shore with Robert. They'd spent a wonderful evening having a picnic in the park before an outdoor movie screen. They hadn't watched an action film or a chick flick this time, but rather a classic oldie instead. It had been a fun and refreshing story, one of those old wartime love stories from long ago. As the last scene faded, closing on a couple kissing on a beach, Robert had taken her hand. "Let's go somewhere," he'd said. "Do you want to?"

"What do you have in mind?" she'd asked him. And when he'd said the beach, Isabel had found it impossible to say no. She loved the majesty and romance of the seashore and always had since she was a kid. It was a four-hour drive, but she didn't mind, as long as she was taking it with him. They'd driven mostly in silence, listening to funky jazz tunes on the radio that caused her heart to pulse in rhythm just at the thought that he was still holding her hand. She had to brave the question, and she knew it. As soon as they got to the shore, she was prepared to ask him. But then they'd gotten there, and everything had been so beautiful as he led her across the dunes and down to an empty stretch of sand.

"You know what I like about being here?" he asked her. "I like the fact that's it's just me and you."

And it was. Not even the gulls were awake at this hour, and all the sand crabs had long since been tucked in. "I like that too," she answered.

He spread his car blanket on the ground and offered her a seat beside him, tucking her under his arm to shield her from the early chill. "Robert," she said as the waves crashed and roared before them, "I've got something to ask you."

"You can ask anything you want. But first, I need to do this…"

When he brought his mouth to hers, Isabel thrilled at the moment. She'd wanted him for so long, and his slow, languorous kiss was like warm molasses on a sultry afternoon. Isabel sighed against him as she kissed him back and he threaded his fingers through her hair.

"You're even prettier than I remembered," he said, gazing down at her. He lightly brushed his lips to hers. "And you're a helluva a lot better kisser too."

"You've improved yourself."

His brow rose in mock offense. "You mean I wasn't good then?"

"You were fine then," she said with a smile, "but you're rocking now."

He growled lightly and pulled her to him. "You don't know how much I want you."

"I want you too," she breathed, even sensing it was wrong with her not fully knowing the truth.

"I think I've always wanted you," he said. "But somehow, with time and space…and life moving on…it's almost like I'd forgotten."

"Yeah."

He kissed her again, then spoke in a husky whisper. "I want to make this work. You and I… We have something, Isabel. Something worth fighting for. I believe that."

"I do too." She met his eyes as the sky streaked purple with the dawn. "But, Robert, I've got to know… Is there somebody else?"

Robert broke their embrace.

"Robert?" she asked, her voice tinged with pain.

He rested his elbows on his knees and hung his head.

"You're the only woman in my heart."

Isabel felt as if a blade had sliced straight through her. "In your heart?"

He took her hand.

"I need you to do something for me. I need you to trust me."

"But what about—?"

"Sometimes life is complicated. More complicated than you know."

"But until tonight, you never… You didn't try to—"

"It wasn't because I didn't want to." He set his eyes on hers. "I've been working on something. A way to make things right. And I'm getting very close. I swear."

"I don't understand."

He looked at her with sad understanding. "I wouldn't expect you to."

She bit her lip and turned away.

"Izzy, please. Look at me."

She slowly turned her gaze to his. "You haven't called me that in a long time."

"I know. But I remember. Remember very clearly what our being together was like."

"What was it like?"

"It was like…magic."

Isabel couldn't argue. What they'd had together as kids had been truly special. Even if their parents had thought of it as puppy love, it had certainly felt like more than that to her and Robert. And now, being here with him, Isabel understood how easy it was for Robert to still exert his power over her. She'd all but forgotten him. Or that was what her head said, anyway. But the truth was, her heart remembered. She recalled the longing in his eyes and the way he used to hold her for hours on end when neither of their parents was home. Her dad had worried about them getting into trouble, and they had. But not in any sort of way nearly as risqué as he might have imagined. They never did much more than kiss and hold each other tight. During a couple of those close-together sessions, Isabel had gotten the idea Robert's body was ready for something more. Though he'd never said so and had never pressed her. Just being with her the way they were seemed good enough. It certainly had been for Isabel. In truth, it had been more than good. It had been wonderful. Theirs was like a storybook love from another realm. Unique and mystical… And yes, it had appeared at the time, most especially *magical.*

"Yeah," she said softly. "It was."

He wrapped her in his arms and tugged her close, his mouth hovering over hers. "I want us to find that magic again," he whispered. "But this time…we need to hold on to it."

Isabel nodded in numb understanding, knowing that she could never fight her feelings for Robert now. Whatever his worries, he was working on a way to sort them out. Isabel had to believe that his feelings for her were sincere and that he'd never intentionally do anything to hurt her. At least, she hoped with her whole heart he wouldn't. Because, at the moment, that heart was brimming with longing and affection for the one guy she now felt she had loved forever.

Robert brought his lips to hers and kissed her sweetly. Then he deepened his passion in a skilled way he'd never known as a boy. Isabel felt herself melting away, losing herself in Robert's embrace and surrendering to his ardor. He pulled her toward him, then gently laid her down, covering her body with his. How she wished they could stay here forever, with ocean breezes rippling and the first morning gulls just starting to call, as he kissed her over and over and her heart lost sight of what was…and could only dream of things to come.

Chapter Five

The next few weeks passed like a dream for Isabel. Though before they'd been seeing each other regularly, since that night on the beach she and Robert had become practically inseparable. She loved everything about him, and being near him was where she wanted to be. It didn't matter if they were out for a fancy dinner or sharing burgers at a drive-through, just being together felt right. Both their academic schedules kept them busy, but they did their best to dovetail their efforts so Isabel's late nights at the studio corresponded with Robert's moonlighting at the lab. One way or another, they'd been able to work things out so they spent nearly every moment of free time each of them had together. For together was where both of them wanted to be.

"*Nooo!*" Isabel yelped as her bowling ball zigzagged across the lane and bounced once more into the alley. "Not again!"

Robert handed her a cold draft beer. "You'll get better with time."

"That's what you said three weeks ago."

He sipped from his own beer and smiled. "I wouldn't worry too much about the bowling. You have other strengths."

"You do too, Doctor," she said, poking him in the ribs.

"I'm not a doctor yet."

She shot him a sexy grin. "No, but you're working on it."

He studied her a long while, emotion filling his eyes. "What do you say we wrap up this game and get out of here?"

"Where do you want to go?"

"Someplace quiet."

A little while later, they sat on a bench in a downtown park, each sipping from decaf coffee. "I can't believe how great it's been seeing you again," she told him.

There was agreement in his eyes. "It's been a pretty special summer."

"And summer's almost over," she said with a sigh.

"Lucky for us we're both enrolled here in the fall."

"Yeah."

"Isabel. I want you to know that, even if we weren't going to be…" He took her hand between them on the bench and turned to face her. "What I mean is, I would have wanted to keep seeing you regardless."

"I would have wanted to keep seeing you too," she said, barely breathing the words.

He set down his cup and brought his palm to her cheek. "I've known this for a long time, but it's taken me a while to get my nerve up to say it. And that's despite the fact I spent…oh, about a million years rehearsing."

"What?"

His face warmed in a smile. "When I was thirteen, I mean. I knew it then. Knew it with my whole heart, but I never told you." He studied her a prolonged beat, his eyes lingering on hers. "I love you, Isabel. Madly and deeply. The truth of the matter is, I don't believe I've ever loved anybody more."

Her heart thumped in response as she felt her face flame. Everything he'd said, she felt as well. She'd adored him long ago, but somehow now—after so much time—she was crazy for him all the more. In a grown-up way, the sort of way that sometimes meant forever.

"Oh, Robert," she said, gazing up at him. "I love you too."

He brought his lips to hers. "That's precisely what I've waited years to hear." Then he kissed her again with the sweetness and passion that had been bottled up from long ago, and Isabel held fast, basking in its glory. While she'd imagined lots of things as a kid, she never could have envisioned being with Robert would be so wonderful. But it was. Wonderful and unforgettable too. Just having him hold her close made everyday cares fade away and her whole world bloom in Technicolor. It was more than special. More than unique. It really *was* like magic.

A few days later, Isabel and Cindy stood beside the punch table, waiting for the server to pour them each another glass. "Another day, another department wedding," Cindy said with a sigh.

"I know," Isabel retorted under her breath. "You wouldn't think there were so many starving artists bent on tying the knot."

"I think it's sweet," Cindy said. "Though in practical terms, I believe you've got the right idea."

Isabel lifted her brow.

"A doctor? Just think of all the art supplies his salary could buy!"

"Just think of all the school loans he'll be repaying," Isabel quipped back.

"I guess you've got a point." She accepted her refilled cup with a nod and turned back to Isabel. "But he won't be repaying them forever."

"I'm not after Robert for the money."

"You're right. There's the body too."

Isabel felt herself blush. "Okay, I'll admit to a bit of physical attraction."

"Only a bit?"

"More than a bit, and you know it."

"Boy, wouldn't I like to. Hey, does he have a brother?"

"Sorry. Only a sister. And she's married."

"Too bad. I was hoping his genes run in the family."

"Want to get some wedding cake?" Isabel asked.

"Sure," Cindy said as they made their way across the room.

As Cindy scarfed down her piece, Isabel neatly wrapped hers in a napkin.

"What on earth are you doing?"

"Saving mine for later."

"You're not hungry?"

"No. I'm hopeful."

"Hopeful of what?"

Isabel lowered her voice in a whisper. "Do you know that old tradition? The one about sleeping with a piece of wedding cake under your pillow?"

"Sounds more like a superstition to me."

"You're supposed to dream of the man you're going to marry."

"Get out. Have you done it before?"

"Only about a billion times. But that was before."

"What do you mean, *before*?"

"Back in the day. When I was a kid. I guess you could say I was something of a wedding-cake junkie."

"No kidding."

Isabel shook her head.

"But you never ate it?"

"Couldn't. That would have been bad luck."

"Now you tell me." Cindy stared down at her empty plate and frowned before looking back up. "So spill it. Who did you dream of? Movie stars? Recording artists? The boy next door?"

"Yeah, *him.*"

"*Him* who?"

"Robert," Isabel said in a whisper. "It was always Robert." She held up a hand in a pledge. "I swear. Only him. Even after he'd moved away."

"Wow. That's impressive. What did you have? Some sort of obsessive disorder?"

Isabel swatted her. "Shut up. I was a kid. A kid with a crush."

Cindy eyed her astutely. "Something tells me you haven't outgrown it."

"Maybe. Maybe not," Isabel said with a toss of her head.

Cindy studied her wrapped-up piece of wedding cake with suspicion. "And what are your plans for that little slice of heaven?"

"I guess I want to see if I still dream of the same angel."

"And if you don't?"

Isabel shrugged and took another swig of punch. "It's just a superstition."

Later that night, Isabel awoke with a gasp. Ramming her hand under her pillow, she found the smashed piece of wedding cake sealed up in a baggie still there. "Well, I'll be…" she said with a happy grin, snuggling back down in bed. The main difference between now and when she was twelve was that this time she'd not just dreamt of a guy with gorgeous brown eyes meeting her at the top of the aisle, she'd also envisioned the honeymoon. A very lovely honeymoon, with lots of vivid detail. *And that Statue-of-David body? Hmm. Yes. I would know it anywhere. In—or out of—a tuxedo.*

Chapter Six

Kip adjusted his hard hat as he stood outside the Kenilworth Building on central campus. He and his capital improvements team were in the midst of erecting a brand-new building to house the growing engineering school, and boy, was it a winner, with all the bells and whistles the administration could hope for. The wealthy alumni benefactors who'd funded this project were bound to be pleased too. They were being given a hard-hat tour of the space tomorrow, and Kip and his senior foreman, Buddy, were putting the rest of the crew through the drill. Which areas were open for touring, and which—due to safety concerns—were still strictly off limits.

Kip said a few words, then turned the floor over to Buddy to address specific questions from the rest of the men. He glanced around, thinking they were lucky to have found this premium location, smack dab between the hospital complex and the high-rise parking garage. The old play house had been torn down to make way. But that was okay. A bigger and more elegant one had been constructed across campus by the arboretum, complete with an outdoor amphitheater. That had come in handy this summer, with the school opening up student performances of Shakespeare to the townsfolk in general. Kip pulled a hanky from his pocket to wipe the building sweat on his brow. Eighty-five degrees in the shade, and it was predicted to get warmer. Apparently, the student body knew it and had dressed accordingly. He perused a group of passing students in shorts and flip-flops as Buddy wrapped up his instructions. Things were a lot less busy here during summer session, but there were still enough kids around to keep the academic atmosphere at play. Kids and a few medical professionals, he mused, as a bunch of young people in scrubs rounded the sidewalk and headed his direction.

Buddy asked him a question, and he turned to address it, believing he'd spotted a familiar face as he did. "That's right," he told his foreman, "nobody in the interior courtyard this time. Not until the skylights are all set and the scaffolding removed."

Not twenty feet behind him, he heard a male voice say, "I can't believe it! You actually heard from Susan?"

But what caused him to set his jaw was the voice Kip heard next. The voice belonging to none other than Isabel's indomitable new boyfriend. "I was starting to think she'd never call. You know what I'm saying? Like maybe I'd dreamed it."

"I hear ya, man," the other one said. "But sometimes dreams *can* come true."

Kip angled his hat and glanced casually over his shoulder. It was Robert Reed all right. Talking one-on-one with some other guy as they trailed behind a group of students.

"This one's been a long time coming, that's for sure," Robert said.

"So when are you going to see her?"

"As soon as she'll let me, I guess." Robert gave a happy chuckle as his voice trailed away, and it was all Kip could do not to wheel around and tackle him. Kip had played football in high school and hadn't forgotten any of those moves. Okay, so maybe he was a little wider in the gut, but his shoulders were still as broad.

And he sure as hell knew how to handle somebody messing with his daughter. Man to man, that's how.

"Kip?" Buddy asked, his face questioning. It was only then that Kip realized he'd missed some sort of question. "What should I tell the guys?"

"You can tell them…" Kip narrowed his eyes toward the sidewalk as Robert and his pal strolled away. "Just wait until they have daughters!" he said with an angry growl.

"Now, Kip," Trudy said on the porch, "I want you to calm down." She'd just poured them a pitcher of lemonade, and at Kip's insistence had also retrieved a bottle of vodka. He dumped some in his pink glass and frowned.

"None it sounds good, Trudy, and you know it."

"Goodness gracious, who knows what you overheard? You could be mistaken."

"About Robert being called by a woman named Susan, and him having a burning itch to see her? A burning itch that…let me guess, here…he likely wants Susan to scratch?"

"You're getting carried away again. For heaven's sakes, Susan could be his sister!"

Kip set down his glass and stared at her. "The Reeds lived beside us for years. You know very well Robert's sister's name is Teresa."

She sighed and sat on the porch swing beside him. "Be that as it may, what you have here is nothing more than idle speculation—over a conversation you weren't even supposed to have overheard."

"Precisely what makes it so damning."

"Or—on the other hand—totally misunderstood."

Kip grunted and refilled his glass.

"I need you to promise me something." Her face was lined with concern. "Promise you won't breathe a word of this to Isabel."

"What? Why?"

"Because, darling," she said calmly, "you don't even know for a fact what's going on. Honestly? Do you want to get Isabel's feelings all stirred up over what could possibly be nothing?"

But if it was nothing, then why did Kip's gut tell him that is was *something*? Something not so good... It was just as he'd suspected all along. Robert Reed wasn't totally what he said he was. Something was up with that boy, something that threatened to upset his daughter. And Kip didn't like it one bit.

"Isabel will be here any moment. She said she's coming with some good news. So let's be the loving, supportive parents and wait and hear what she has to say, why don't we?"

He set his jaw.

"Kip... Please promise me, honey. Not a word."

Just then, Isabel's sweet voice called from the foyer. "Mom? Dad? Anybody home?"

"We're on the porch, dear!" Trudy called. She brought her finger to her lips in a silencing motion, and Kip harrumphed.

A few seconds later, Isabel pressed through the kitchen's screen door. "I have great news," she said, her face full of sunshine. "My work's been accepted at the opening!"

Trudy squealed and stood to hug her. "That's wonderful, baby!"

Kip stood, offering a congratulatory hug as well. "Is this the art show you were after? The big one at the Smith Center?"

"The biggest one in town," Isabel said with a proud grin. "What's more, I get to curate the show!"

"What's that mean?" Kip asked Trudy in a whisper.

"She gets to put it together," Trudy answered back.

"That sounds very impressive," Kip said, his chest welling with pride. "We're so proud of you, sweetheart. When is the special day?"

"Next Friday," she said with a smile. "And it's going to be a really fancy affair. Cocktail dresses and wine. A caterer and everything."

Trudy oohed and ahhed, apparently liking the sound of this.

"Of course, you're both invited."

"Will Robert be there?" Kip asked.

"Of course he will," Trudy said, like that was the silliest question.

Isabel's dainty face drooped in a frown. "Actually," she said, "he won't."

"Why not?" Kip pressed.

"Oh, that's right," Trudy butted in. "Friday's his night at the lab."

"It's not that." She met her parents' expectant faces. "He's going out of town."

"*Out of town?*" Kip's deep tenor rose a decibel, and Trudy laid a hand on his forearm.

"It seems he has some kind of business in New York."

Kip opened his mouth to speak, and Trudy tightened the grip of her fingers. Kip winced and zipped his lip. Totally against his better judgment, but to avoid fireworks with his wife later.

"We're very sorry about that, dear," Trudy said. "We know you must be disappointed."

"Yeah," Isabel answered. "I am. But I guess the timing couldn't be helped."

Robert walked Isabel home after they'd shared a late lunch. It was Thursday afternoon, and he'd be leaving for the airport soon. "I'm really sorry about missing your opening. If there was any way in the world to change the timing of my trip, I would."

"But you can't."

"I've waited for this day forever. But, in all honesty, I didn't get to pick it."

"I wish you could tell me where you're going."

"New York."

"I meant, why."

As they approached her building, Robert stopped, taking her in his arms. "I hope you believe me when I say the *why* has a whole lot to do with you."

"I want to believe," she said, looking up at him.

"Then do." He kissed her softly. "I've been through some stuff, Isabel. But my whole world is about to change, and when it does, I want you in it."

"Then why won't you tell me?"

"Because, Izzy." He reached forward and thumbed her nose. "I don't want to jinx it. Don't want to take any chance of things going wrong. But when I turn them around, and everything's right, you'll be the first one to know. I can promise you that."

"When are you coming home?"

"Just as soon as I can," he said, pulling her close.

Chapter Seven

Isabel was nervous but excited. Her big night had at long last arrived. She'd managed to orchestrate this show highlighting an array of graduate students' work, while speaking to a unified theme about preserving nature in the environment. The installations here were awe-inspiring and innovative, and Isabel was pleased she'd played a part in pulling the disparate—yet interesting—displays together. She hadn't had much time to survey students in the department and canvass entries relating to her chosen topic. But it had all come together for her somehow. And the flash of inspiration had left her breathless at its outcome.

"Fabulous work," her favorite instructor told her. "Inspiring."

Isabel beamed from ear to ear as appreciative arts patrons flooded the main gallery. "Thanks for giving me this chance."

"There's no one who deserves it more than you," Elizabeth said. "You have promise, Isabel, and a keen eye. Not just as an artist but as a curator too."

Isabel hoped that was true. While she wanted to pursue her own art, she also understood she'd need to put bread on the table. Curatorial practices was not a bad field, and one to which she was establishing entrees from the likes of Elizabeth and several of her contacts, to whom Elizabeth had been kind enough to introduce her.

"Oh look!" she told her teacher. "There are my parents."

"Why don't you go on over and say hello?" Elizabeth urged.

Isabel carried her glass of Chablis in their direction, feeling every bit the sophisticate that she'd aspired to be. Imagine! Her own opening! And at a well-known gallery besides. Just because it held a university affiliation didn't make it any less important. Competition in the arts was keen these days, and Isabel knew it. She was just so very grateful to have been given this opportunity to make some meager inroads.

"Mom, Dad," she said, crossing to them with an open-armed hug. "Thanks so much for coming."

"We wouldn't have missed it," her dad said.

Her mom smiled fondly. "We're so proud of you, Isabel."

Kip nodded. "Yes. We are."

"Come on and let me get you both a glass of wine. Then I'll show you around."

Kip laid another small sandwich on his plate and surreptitiously surveyed the art before him. There sure seemed to be a lot of nudies here. Then again, that had been passing for art since the old days. He chomped on the tiny triangle and wrinkled his nose. Why did this taste like he'd just sampled a salad with ranch dressing?

Trudy, who walked ahead, her armed linked in Isabel's, smiled over her shoulder. "I'm proud of you, Kip. Going for the whole-wheat veggie sandwiches. Very sound."

Kip stared down at the offending crudité in horror. No wonder it was so terrible. It was good for him! He quickly scanned the room, then slid his sandwich remains onto a passing tray, which carted off dirty dishes. Isabel shared a laugh with her mom, then glanced back at him.

"Finished already? That's great, Dad. Why don't you go and get some more?"

Yeah, maybe he'd do that. He'd spied some meatballs in the buffet that looked a lot more his speed.

"And load up on the meatballs!" Isabel chirped as if reading his mind. "They're vegan!"

Kip stopped halfway to the buffet table and grunted. He knew they should have stopped to eat before coming here, but Trudy had protested there'd be plenty of food. Like any of this healthy stuff counted. The line ahead of him moved along, and Kip spotted something intriguing. To his delight, it was a vat of miniature hotdogs drenched in what smelled like a delicious bourbon sauce. "Those aren't tofu?" he asked the caterer, who was resetting the tea lights beneath the various pans.

"One hundred percent all beef."

Kip sighed with relief and piled his plate high, thinking if this was what it took to get through the night without his stomach grumbling, he'd do it. Isabel still had to give her speech introducing the guest artists, and he supposed that afterwards, he and Trudy would be expected to mingle some more. He poked a wiener with a toothpick, then popped it in his mouth. *Mmmm, succulent.* A split-second later he nearly spit it back out, unable to believe what he was seeing. It was Robert! In the all-together. Just as naked as the day he was born, the colorful canvass centered right behind the hot dogs, of all things. *Miniature hot dogs,* Kip reminded himself. He carted his plate toward the canvas to get a closer look, realizing that Robert's attributes more than measured up. Kip set down his plate on a nearby cart, suddenly losing his appetite.

"Wonderful, isn't it?" A woman wearing a name tag that read *Elizabeth* asked him. "I believe that's Isabel's most promising work."

"Isabel?" Kip felt the blood drain from his face.

"She's our featured artist tonight," the woman explained, "and this exhibit's curator." She studied him a moment, her face lighting up. "Say, aren't you Mr. Miller?"

"Your father's taking an awfully long time getting his food," Trudy told Isabel. "I'll go see what's keeping him." Just then a couple of arts patrons approached, wanting to offer their congratulations to Isabel. After a brief introduction, Trudy excused herself and made for the bar, where Kip stood pouring two glasses of wine.

"That's sweet of you, dear," Trudy said, assuming one of them was for her. "But I haven't even finished my first yet."

Without saying a word, Kip downed one, then set it on the table. "These are both for me."

"But what…?"

He motioned with the second glass still in his hand, and Trudy's gaze traveled across the room. "Oh my!" she said, her gaze falling on the picture. She stepped a little closer as Kip trailed her. "Is that Robert?"

"In the flesh," Kip answered dryly.

Trudy nursed her wine and considered the portrait. "Well, well. He certainly *has* grown up."

"Trudy!" Kip scolded. "Watch yourself."

"I'm just saying—"

"I know what you're saying. He's no longer Mr. Little Bitty from next door. He's got the whole Oscar Mayer thing going on."

"Kip!"

"I see you two found my painting," Isabel said, approaching.

Trudy shot Kip a warning look, telling him to hold his tongue.

"Yes, dear," Trudy said sweetly. "You did...mighty good work."

Isabel sighed at the portrait. "It helped that I had a mighty good model."

Kip's temples pulsed so hard he feared his whole face might explode. "I just have one question." Trudy stealthily pinched him, but he continued anyway. "Did he pose for the whole class, or was it a private sitting?"

Two and a half hours later, Trudy and Kip exited the Smith Center. He plucked a hanky from his pocket to wipe his brow, not knowing how he'd lived through it. His only daughter was not only involved with some leech with a treacherous secret, she'd been painting nudie pictures of him too! Kip didn't know how, but things seemed to have gone from bad to worse. In fact, he didn't see how they could get any more abysmal. That was what he thought until he saw Robert stepping to the curb from a cab.

Trudy tugged on his elbow, apparently having seen Robert as well. "I want you to remember yourself," she said. "And think of your daughter. This is her night, sweetheart. We wouldn't want to do anything to ruin it."

They descended the granite stairs and met Robert halfway as he ascended. "Mr. and Mrs. Miller," he said with surprise.

"It's nice to see you, Robert," Trudy said. "We didn't think you could make it."

"Almost didn't," he said, a bit winded. "Got a last-minute flight back and had to hightail it here from the airport."

"Where were you again?" Kip asked, purposely oblivious.

Robert's gaze darted to the museum entrance, then settled on his again. "New York."

"We knew that, Kip," Trudy said mildly. "Let's move along."

But Kip stayed planted in place like a pillar. "And what, pray tell, were you doing in New York? *Seeing someone?*" Trudy tugged at his arm as Robert blinked hard.

"Sir, I can explain—"

"So you weren't seeing Susan?"

"I'm sure she's just a friend," Trudy inserted.

"No, ma'am, an attorney."

"Attorney?" Kip parroted. "What's this? My artist daughter isn't good enough for you?"

"No, sir. I mean, yes, sir. Isabel is plenty good enough. Way too good for me, in fact."

Kip glared at him. "You've got that part right."

Robert steeled his nerves and barreled ahead. "The truth is I went there because I had to. I had something important to take care of. Get out of, I mean."

Trudy's face creased with worry. "A previous engagement?"

"No, ma'am." He glanced at Kip and flinched as if anticipating a blow. "My marriage."

That was the last word he heard before Kip's top blew off. The next thing Robert knew, Kip had tackled him to the steps and had corralled him by the collar.

"Kip! What are you doing?" Trudy yelped.

"What I should have done ages ago!" Kip hollered. He tugged Robert up toward him by his lapels. "You mean to tell me that all this time—the whole time you've been seeing Isabel—you were *married* to somebody else?"

"Technically, yes, but—"

"Were you or weren't you, Robert?" Trudy asked in shock.

"I'm sorry, Mrs. Miller," he said, his face beet red. "I apologize for lying to both of you. But it's really not like you— *Ow!*"

Kip yanked him forward to spew out the words, "*You had the nerve to come into my house...? To deceive not just Isabel, but all of us?*" He glanced at Trudy, who appeared faint. "We have to tell Isabel."

"I'm going to tell her," Robert squawked. "I was on my way just now!"

"Kip," Trudy said. "He's right. This is for the two of them to work out."

Kip would prefer to work things out right here and now. Mano a mano with Robert, that little pipsqueak. But he knew that his wife wouldn't forgive him. Isabel, God love her, might even get angry with him too. Though if she asked her dad to settle things up with Robert later, he'd be more than happy to do it. He felt Trudy's hand on his shoulder and released his grip, leaving a stunned Robert to fall back on his elbows. "*You!*" he said with a parting growl. "*Stay away from my daughter!*"

As they left, Trudy glanced sadly over her shoulder. "You really disappointed us, Robert. And I was one of the ones pulling for you."

Chapter Eight

Robert stood on wobbly knees and dusted off his dress slacks. He watched Kip and Trudy walk away, shaking their heads as they made for their car. Of all the scenarios Robert had envisioned occurring this evening, Kip's assault hadn't been among them. Though Robert knew he couldn't entirely blame Kip for reacting the way he did. Robert understood the information had come as a shock. He worried it would come as one to Isabel as well. He only hoped she'd give him more time than her dad had for him to explain the entire truth.

Robert straightened his tie and pulled back the heavy door, finding the museum's entry foyer nearly empty. Only a few scattered guests remained, chatting casually amidst the catering staff that was busily cleaning up. It took him a few moments to find Isabel in a back chamber, gathering up some extra programs. She heard his approach and looked up. "Robert!" she said, her cheeks flushed. She was stunning in a short black dress and heels, her blonde curls twisted up in a knot behind her. She set down her pile of papers and hurried to him. "I didn't think you could make it."

He sadly surveyed the empty room, then took her in his arms. "Looks like I missed it."

"Most of it, yeah." She gave him a tilted smile, and his heart stilled. How he wished there was a way to make things easy, but any way he could think of was hard.

She ran her hand down his lapel, noting the tear at his collar. "What happened to your shirt?"

"Let's just say I had a little run-in with Kip on my way here."

"With my dad?" she asked with surprise. "I don't understand."

He looked down into trusting blue eyes, hating to shatter her illusions. But the only way to move forward at this point was with full disclosure, and Robert knew it. "I told him, Isabel. Told him why I went to New York."

Her delicate brow wrinkled in concern. "And now you're going to tell me?"

"All I ask is that you hear me out. Let me say my whole piece."

"Robert," she said, her voice trembling. "You're scaring me."

He drew a deep breath, then released it, gathering his courage. He locked on her gaze and willed the words from his throat, but they wouldn't come.

"What is it? What's happened?"

"When I told you before there was no one else, that wasn't exactly right."

"What?"

"Isabel, I'm married."

She pushed back in his arms and broke their embrace. "*Married?*" she shrieked, looking as if she'd been slapped across the face.

"But it's not like you think!"

She shook her head in disbelief and then stammered, "You mean, all this time… When you and I have been together?" She brought her hand to her mouth as if she might retch.

"Isabel." Robert stepped forward, but she inched back.

"Stay where you are."

"You don't understand. I've been trying to get it undone."

"Sure you have," she said, clearly not believing him. "That's what they all say, isn't it?"

"They?"

"Men, Robert! Like you!" She shot him an accusing glare. "And all this time I blamed my dad, said he was overreacting…" She stood up straighter and squared her shoulders. "But he was right, wasn't he? You weren't to be trusted. All this time, you've been married to somebody else."

"Yes, but—"

"Were you or weren't you?"

Robert hung his head. "I was."

"Does she know about me?"

"No."

"Perfect. That's perfect."

"My marriage was over a long time ago."

She set a hand on her hip and asked combatively, "What do you think, Robert? That I don't go to the movies? If that isn't the oldest line in the book, then I don't know—"

"She left me, Isabel," he said, his voice cracking. Fire welled in his eyes, and his jaw trembled. "Ran out on me, don't you know."

She gasped and blinked at him. "What?"

"Seven years ago, to be exact. We were barely even married. We got married right out of college, and it scarcely lasted six months. Six months was all we had before she put me through seven years of hell."

Isabel brought her hands to her head, a million emotions swirling inside her. "I'm not getting any of this," she whimpered as tears sprang from her eyes. "Except for the part about you being married."

"But not for long. At the stroke of midnight, it's over." He held her gaze, dark eyes sincere. "That's what I've been trying to tell you. My meeting in New York was with my attorney, Susan. She's the one who called that night when we were out to dinner."

Isabel lifted a hand to wipe back her tears. "I'm listening."

He heaved a breath, his shoulders sagging. "Jenny left without so much as a word. I didn't even see it coming."

"Then how—?"

"She left a note by the coffeepot in the kitchen. *Going to Florence to find myself.*"

"Oh!"

"Yeah, it wasn't the nicest birthday gift I'd received."

"She did that on your birthday?" Isabel asked, unable to believe the callousness of it.

"To be honest, I'm not sure she remembered what day it was. I guess all she was thinking about was leaving."

Isabel stared at him, her heart softening. Of all the people to do that to, Robert surely hadn't deserved it. Even if the marriage had been bad or things had started to sour between them, Isabel couldn't imagine what would drive a woman to do something so cold. No matter how hard it had been hearing Robert's confession, in her heart Isabel believed that he was speaking the truth. The pain was written in his eyes, just at the mention of what was bound to be an awful memory. "I'm sorry."

"The worst part was, because she did things the way she did—leaving the country and all—this left me in a terrible predicament."

"How long was she gone?"

Robert slowly shook his head. "She's still gone."

Another scenario occurred. "How do you know she's okay? That maybe she didn't get hurt?"

"We have mutual friends who've seen her around. Sipping cappuccino in a café in Venice… Out to dinner with a gaggle of girlfriends in Rome. Jenny's apparently having the time of her life as an ex-pat and has absolutely no intention of coming home. I've tried contacting her over the years, having my lawyer send official correspondence. She's ignored all of it."

"Well then, how can you…" Isabel swallowed hard, hating to hear herself say it. "Get a divorce?"

"There's a seven-year abandonment rule. That is, if you have some way to prove it."

"The note by the coffeepot?"

"In court, that could prove ambiguous. She didn't precisely say she wasn't coming back." He paused a moment for effect. "But in the postcard she did."

"Postcard?"

"Two months after she'd gone, I got a postcard from Pisa. *Having the time of my life. Decided to stay. You can keep condo and my cat.*"

"Cat?" Isabel asked in shock.

"No worries. Her sister took it."

"So this postcard…? It was proof?"

"Postmarked seven years ago today."

The art deco clock in the atrium began to chime.

"What's that?"

"Perelli's clock," she said. "The one in there." Her gaze travelled to the next room, the truth slowly dawning.

Robert caught his breath. "Isabel, what time is it?"

"When my folks left, it was after eleven."

The clock struck again, then again, and again.

"How many was that?" he asked.

"Ten, I think."

"I can't believe it." Robert felt awash in relief. It was if he'd been drowning for seven long years and someone—at long last—had thrown him a life raft. "Isabel…" he said as the clock chimed eleven.

"Robert?" she asked, blue eyes wide.

And then, miracle of miracles, it happened. The clock chimed midnight. It was over.

He ran his hands through his hair, unable to absorb the moment. After all this time and the endless court battles… False starts and disappointments. At least three times before, Robert had believed himself on the brink of divorce. But each time, some unforeseen legal precedent had blocked it. Susan had assured him that *abandonment* was their big ticket. It might take longer to work through than the other strategies they'd tried, but according to her, it was the best thing they had. They'd win this battle for his freedom at last. After so long of holding on, Robert had almost lost faith in a hopeful outcome. Now, incredibly, it had arrived.

Isabel brought a hand to her heart. "What does this mean?"

"I'm a free man."

Isabel steadied herself on shaky knees as the waves of these truths crashed over her. First he was married… Now he wasn't?

"Are you okay?" he asked, walking to her. "You look a little pale."

She stunned him by latching on to his coat lapels, and for a crazy instant, Robert feared she might tackle him to the ground just as her dad had. "So you're saying…" She gripped tighter and pulled him toward her. "You're…*not*…married? To anyone? Anymore?"

He vehemently shook his head. "That's the good news," he said with a squeak.

She narrowed her gaze, and his heart thumped in his chest. "And you didn't tell me before *because*…?"

"I wasn't sure how you would take it. Plus…"

She cinched his lapels in her hands and pulled him right up against her as she stood on tiptoes to stare into his eyes. "Plus what?"

"Oh God, Izzy. I didn't want to jinx it. I'd wanted out of that marriage for a while, but after I met you, I became desperate to leave it. I didn't tell you because I was still working things out. I didn't want you to worry. Have you agonizing and waiting over some timeline only to have some last-minute thing go wrong. I couldn't put you through that. Wading through the abysmal legal maneuvers. Watching and hoping for it all to be done. Becoming painfully disappointed time and again.

"I apologize if I screwed up by handling things this way, but you've got to believe that I never meant to hurt you. I would never…in a million years…hurt you. I care for you far too much."

She relaxed her grip but still held on.

"You've got to trust me when I say there's never been anyone but you. When I saw you again that day on campus, it was all over for me. You're the only one I want, Izzy. In some ways, I see now that you're the only one I've always wanted. Please, say something."

"You know, Robert Reed, you're making me crazy with this." Tears leaked from her eyes, but she smiled softly just the same. "He loves me, he loves me not..."

"Isabel," he said, steadying her against him. "You're not hearing me. I said, I've *always* loved you. The heart remembers. At least this one does."

He looked deep in her eyes, and her whole world went off-kilter. He had to be telling the truth. The Robert she knew had never been much of a liar, not even as a kid. And he was all grown up now, and strong enough to hold her—even though her legs seemed to be giving way. He'd turned her emotions inside out with his confession, but the words that she hung on to were the ones that spelled forever. Robert did love her; she was sure of it. Whatever had gone before was over now. And if it wasn't, the two of them would deal with it together. For together with Robert was where she'd always longed to be. She tilted her chin toward his, her lips trembling.

"You're the only one I've ever wanted too."

"I was so hoping you'd say that."

Then he claimed her mouth with his and swept her away with his kiss.

Chapter Nine

Isabel sat beside her mother on the porch swing while Kip perched in a rattan chair nearby. "I don't see why I have to talk to Robert," he said, feeling grumpy.

"You don't," Trudy said, her dainty shoes rocking back and forth. "All you have to do is listen."

"And remember." Isabel studied him sternly. "You promised to be nice."

Kip didn't like being cornered, and this corralling was among the worst of them. Something was going on here, something that had his wife and daughter in cahoots, Robert in the know, and Kip on the outside. "You already explained all about his ex-wife," he said to Isabel. "Why do I need to hear the same story again from him?"

Trudy and Isabel innocently looked at each other and shrugged. "Maybe he wants to tell it to you man to man," Trudy offered.

"That's right," Isabel inserted. "Clear the air."

If there was an air clearing about to go down, then why did it appear the two women in his life were throwing up a smoke screen?

"I think I hear a car!" Isabel said, getting to her feet.

"Why don't we all go and greet him?" Trudy said, standing as well.

Kip reluctantly followed after them, hoping this whole thing would be over soon. He had a ball game to watch and other things to attend to. Important things, like rearranging his CD collection or helping Trudy sort those blasted cookbooks.

"Sir," Robert said with a nod. "It's good to see you."

He wished he could say the same, but the truth was he still wasn't over it. That whole marriage thing had sat with him the wrong way. If a man can hide one thing, he can hide something else. That was the trouble with deception. Some people didn't know where to stop. He suspiciously rolled his eyes toward Trudy, who was grinning like a cat who'd swallowed a canary. The entire thing, feathers and all. "It's a beautiful day," she offered. "Isabel and I were thinking it would be nice if you boys took a walk."

"A walk?" Kip's tone rose in dismay. To add insult to injury, now he had to exercise? Didn't he get enough of that at work, walking around, supervising everything? Standing on his feet nine to ten hours a day?

"Go on," Trudy said, giving him a little push down the path. He begrudgingly sidled up next to Robert but kept his distance. Arm's length. So he wouldn't be tempted to reach up and throttle the boy the way he'd nearly done before.

"We'll be back in a bit," Robert told the ladies with an easy grin.

Why did Kip have the feeling that everyone else around here knew something he didn't?

Robert started right in on it before they had even rounded the corner. "Thanks for agreeing to talk with me today, sir."

"I'm not sure I was given much of a choice." He glanced back at the women, who watched them expectantly. Trudy motioned him forward with her hand, urging him along.

"The truth is, I wanted to talk to you about Isabel."

"Listen, Robert, if this is about that whole Susan thing, I know all about it. Isabel and Trudy filled me in."

"I know it might seem hard to understand."

"It's not really for me to understand or not, is it?" He shot Robert a sideways glance. "That's up to Isabel."

"Yes, sir. I agree, sir. And she does too. It was a shock to her at first as well. But once I explained it—"

Kip blew a hard breath and stopped walking. "Robert," he said, meeting the young man's eyes. "What's this really about?"

Robert stunned him by throwing himself down on one knee. "Sir, I want to marry your daughter!"

Kip nervously scanned the block, then hissed under his breath. Of all things, Mrs. Meryl was out watering her petunias, and she was staring at them, mouth agape. "What are you doing?"

Robert latched on to his arm. "Asking for Isabel's hand."

Kip stared down at the boy in horror and shook off his hold. "Her *what*? Get up!" he said in a hoarse whisper. "The neighbors are staring." He grabbed Robert under his arm and yanked him to his feet. Robert shielded his face like he feared Kip was going to slug him.

"Now what are you doing?" Kip spouted in low tones.

"Self-defense?"

"And *you* have the balls to ask to marry my daughter?" Kip huffed and stormed forward.

"I didn't have to do it," Robert called after him.

Kip slowly turned on his heels. "What did you say?"

Robert unabashedly met his eyes. "I said I didn't have to do it. Go to the trouble of asking for her hand. I want your blessing, sir. Yours and Mrs. Miller's both. But even if I don't get it, I'm planning to ask her."

"Harrumph."

"You just told me yourself, Isabel makes up her own mind."

Kip hung his head, wondering where he'd gone wrong. Maybe this had to do with the last time he went to confession. It had been so long ago, he couldn't even recall when that was. This was divine retribution, and he knew it. What else could it be?

"Mr. Miller."

Kip slowly looked up.

"I might not have done everything right in your eyes, but I can assure you of one thing: I desperately love your daughter. I am madly and unconditionally, one hundred percent, without a shadow of a doubt in love with her, and I will do everything in my power to make her happy." After a pause, he continued. "I also know how much Isabel loves you. And part of my making her happy involves finding a way for you and me to get along. I really want that, Mr. Miller. For all of us to be a family. Because I know that's what Isabel would want."

Kip swallowed hard, thinking of the speech he'd given to Trudy's father. A speech not so different from this one, delivered to a man who couldn't stand the sight of him and abhorred the thought of someone as lowly as a construction foreman marrying his only daughter. It had taken Brad years to accept him. Even after Kip had started his own business and bought Trudy the big house, Brad wouldn't stop by to visit. It was only after Isabel was born that Brad had finally started to soften. Isabel, Kip saw, could melt the heart of any man. Including this one standing before him here.

"You really do love her, don't you, boy?"

"With my whole heart."

Kip perused him a beat, his own heart telling him the truth. His Isabel loved Robert too. "Then do your best not to muck it up."

"Sir?" Robert asked in surprise.

"The proposal."

A few days later, Robert called to ask Isabel on a special date. What was special about it was that he wouldn't tell her where they were going. He'd also been less than forthright about the discussion he'd had with her father. Trudy hadn't been able to get a word out of Kip either. In a strange way, it was as if the two men had formed a pact. Isabel and her mom hadn't even realized men could be that way. *So sneaky.* Something was up for sure. But, whatever it was, it couldn't spell gloom and doom. Her dad seemed far too chipper as of late. And why on earth was he sorting his CDs in a way to single out dancing music?

Robert held back the door as Isabel stepped into the car. "Your carriage awaits."

She eyed him curiously as he skirted around the car and took his own place in the driver seat. "Still won't say where we're going?" she asked when he took his seat beside her.

"On a picnic." He beamed, patting the basket in the backseat. It was late in the day, and the sun was just setting.

"On the beach?" she asked, hopeful.

"Better."

After a bit, Isabel realized they were driving north, headed toward her old neighborhood.

"Robert?" she asked uncertainly. "Don't tell me this is a double date with my parents."

"Nope, sweetheart." He winked, and her tailbone tingled. "This night was meant for you and me."

Soon they were through the gate to her old neighborhood, and Isabel understood. Robert was taking her to his favorite place. That spot overlooking the valley where he used to go as a kid.

"My lady," he said, opening her door and helping her out of the car.

"You're being awfully chivalrous tonight," she said, arching an eyebrow.

He opened the back door of the car and pulled out the picnic basket. "That's because I'm out with a princess."

"Let's see…" she said, flirting. "That would make you…a prince?"

"Don't make me get out my sword and show it to you."

"Robert!" she said with a laugh, but her heart was light.

"Come on." He took her hand. "The sun's just going down."

She let him lead her up the winding path that snaked through falling shadows. This was so romantic, just the two of them stealing away. Even though it was in her old neighborhood, she couldn't help but feel a bit reckless. Like she was sneaking off in the night with some forbidden guy. They climbed up on that old, flat-topped rock with the magnificent view of the city, even more majestic now with the sky streaking purple and grenadine.

"I hope this is all right?" he asked her.

"It's perfect." She helped him spread the blanket, then took a seat.

"Hungry?" he asked, settling down beside her.

"A little."

He rummaged in the basket and handed her half a baguette.

"What's this?"

"Cheese sandwich."

Isabel laughed at the memory. As kids, that was what they threatened to pack when the two of them ran away. They often made plans to run away together, but Isabel never truly thought it would come to pass. "This is pretty elegant cheese," she said, peeking between the bread layers. "And, oh! What's that?"

"Brie and prosciutto." He pulled one from the basket for himself, unwrapped it, and took a hearty bite. "Since we're adults now, I thought I'd step it up."

Isabel nodded, taking a nibble of hers. Boy, was it good. Better than any old slice of cheddar on white bread for certain.

"Can I pour you a drink?"

"A drink would be great."

To her surprise, he extracted a bottle of expensive champagne. "Really going high-class tonight, huh?"

"Only the best for the best," he said, popping the bottle open.

The cork arced through the air and flew off the rock, catapulting into the valley below them. Isabel giggled. "You're a lot of good fun, you know that?"

"Good fun?"

"Yeah," she said, feeling her face warm all over. "Great to be with. I don't know... It's like... Like I never have to worry too much about what to do or say. All I have to do is be myself."

He filled a plastic cup with bubbly and handed it to her. "That's the way I like you."

After he filled his own cup, she raised hers in a toast. "That's the way I like you too."

"Chips?" he offered, pulling out a bag.

"I'm glad you didn't worry about packing healthy."

"Hey!" he protested. "These are *all natural*. See?"

Isabel felt as light and breezy as the late August winds blowing around them. She'd had the very best summer with Robert. One she'd never forget. They sat in companionable silence, both enjoying their food and the view. After a while, Robert packed away the remnants of their dinner, but not the champagne.

"You know what I like about this spot?" he asked her. "I like the fact that it's always been here for me."

"What do you mean?"

"If these hills had ears…" he said with a laugh.

"Oh?" she asked, looking over at him. "What would they hear?"

"Probably an earful about one special girl." He looked wistfully over the valley. "*Isabel… Isabel… Isabel…* That was her name. If you listen closely enough, you can probably still hear the echo."

"Go on," she said, nudging his arm.

"Okay, I will." He swallowed hard and set down his champagne. "Isabel," he said as night grew nigh. "I have something to tell you. A confession to make."

She watched his eyes, dark embers in the lengthening dusk. "Yes?"

"When I was, oh, about…" He stretched his hand high above the rock in front of him. "Yay high."

"What?"

"Okay," he admitted. "Maybe I was a little taller. But, hey, the important thing is it was a long time ago."

Isabel's heart skipped a beat as she wondered where this was going.

"I was thirteen, in any case."

"I liked you a lot at thirteen," she said in a low whisper.

"Yeah," he answered. "I liked you a lot too. We shared a lot of things between us, kept some pretty good secrets. But there's one thing I never told you."

She looked at him expectantly.

"I never told you about this."

"This place? No, you didn't." She looked around at the gorgeous scenery. "Why not?"

He pursed his lips a beat, then sweetly stroked back her hair. "Because...this is where I'd planned to take you."

"Take me?"

"Once I'd saved up enough money...and grown into a man, I suppose. I couldn't think of a quicker way to do it. But I did know I'd want to. The fact of the matter is, I spent a hell of a lot of time practicing up."

To her amazement, Robert pulled a small box from the picnic basket.

"I want you to know that it's true. You're the first girl I loved and actually wanted to marry. I asked you over and over again... Right up here on this rock."

"What did I say?"

His eyes twinkled. "You always said yes."

He flipped open the ring box, and Isabel covered her mouth with a gasp. A beautiful solitaire glistened in the rising moonlight. "Isabel Miller," he said, taking her hand, "my sweet, long-lost Izzy. Swear to me you'll never be lost again. We fell away from each other one time, through no fault of our own. But now that fate has brought us back together, I can't imagine my life going on without you." He took the ring and positioned it over her finger. "Say that you'll be mine. For as long as we both shall live."

He met her eyes, and Isabel's heart rose in her throat.

"Be my bride."

Isabel didn't know if it had started to rain or whether those were tears streaming down her cheeks. She nodded, and Robert's face opened up in a rainbow. He slid the ring on her finger and kissed her soundly. "I love you, baby," he said in a husky whisper. "I always will."

"I'll always love you too," she returned. "I probably always have."

He took her in his arms then, knocking over the champagne, but neither one cared. They just stayed locked in a tight embrace, each sensing the rhythm of the other one's heart. It was just like it used to be, only better. And nothing could be better than this. Isabel was so happy, she felt she could fly, straight up to the moon and past the third star…straight on till morning.

"You'll always be my girl," he said, holding her close. And, in her heart, Isabel knew that she would.

"That's the only way I'd have it," she said, hugging him back.

Epilogue

Cindy sat beside Trudy at the head table. Both were dressed in elegant attire.

"I want to thank you for helping organize the wedding," Trudy told her. "It was a beautiful affair, and you were a lovely maid of honor."

"Isabel was a beautiful bride," Cindy said, motioning with her champagne flute toward the dance floor.

Isabel and Kip were enjoying the traditional father-daughter dance, while Robert waited in the wings, prepared to take over.

"She certainly is," Trudy said with a smile. "You know," she said to Cindy, "I don't believe I've ever seen Kip so happy."

"What happened to the overprotective dad?"

"I guess he grew up."

"Yeah," Cindy said with a longing look at the happy couple. "I suppose a lot of people did."

On the dance floor, Kip gathered Isabel and her billowy gown in his arms. It seemed an eternity he'd waited for this day. Waited for it and dreaded it both. For the main thing he feared was that Isabel wouldn't find somebody good enough. Someone to love and care for her in the special way that Kip hoped. Now that she had, Kip's spirit had lightened. Robert was a good man. A man who deeply loved his daughter. He would look after her, Kip was sure of it. And nothing gave him greater peace.

"Dad," she said, looking up at him, her eyes a beautiful blue. "I want to thank you for this day. For everything."

"I'm glad you're happy," he said, holding her close. Then he swirled her around, those old memories flooding back. Cradling Isabel as a baby... Isabel dancing on his shoes at his cousin's wedding... Isabel beaming in his arms in her first communion dress... Isabel in her graduation cap and gown... And now, Isabel the beautiful bride, about to leave his arms forever.

Robert approached, and Kip graciously stepped aside. "Take care of my baby girl," he said in a hoarse whisper.

"I will, sir," Robert assured him.

Kip passed off Isabel as she gave them a laugh. "Come on, guys," she said, rolling her eyes. "*I* can take care of myself."

"I believe that," Robert said, taking her in his arms.

"Then you've learned a lot already." Kip studied him with admiration, then walked away.

"What did you two talk about on that walk?" Isabel asked Robert beneath the sway of the music.

"Oh, you know... Stuff."

"Stuff?" Isabel playfully swatted his shoulder. "Fine. Keep your little secret."

Robert thoughtfully watched Kip pull Trudy onto the dance floor. Even after all their years together, when Kip looked at Trudy, she still blushed like a bride. "Something tells me I could learn a lot from your father."

"What?"

"He won the love of two terrific women. That says something."

Isabel grinned broadly. "Yeah. It says a lot."

"Will you promise me something?"

"Anything you wish."

"Promise that you'll go easy on me…if we have a daughter."

"What do you mean?"

"It's nothing, really," he said, studying Kip and Trudy from across the room. "It's just that I guess I'm starting to understand your dad."

"Robert Reed," she scolded, "swear to me you won't be that impossible."

He held her close, kissing the top of her head. "Sorry, Izzy. Can't promise you that."

The End

A Note from the Author

Thanks for reading *The Wedding Wish*. I hope you enjoyed it. If you did, please help other people find this book.

1. This book is lendable, so loan it to a friend who you think might like it so that she (or he) can discover me, too.

2. Help other people find this book: write a review.

3. Sign up for my newsletter so that that you can learn about the next book as soon as it's available. Write to GinnyBairdRomance@gmail.com with "newsletter" in the subject heading.

4. Come like my Facebook page: http://www.facebook.com/GinnyBairdRomance.

5. Comment on my blog: The Story Behind the Story at http://www.goodreads.com.

6. Visit my website: http://www.ginnybairdromance.com for details on other books available at multiple outlets now.